Marcus Blakey Allmond

Estelle

Marcus Blakey Allmond

Estelle

ISBN/EAN: 9783337370619

Printed in Europe, USA, Canada, Australia, Japan

Cover: Foto ©Andreas Hilbeck / pixelio.de

More available books at **www.hansebooks.com**

ESTELLE

AN IDYL OF OLD VIRGINIA

BY

MARCUS BLAKEY ALLMOND, A.M., LL.D.

Magazine Medalist, University of Virginia; Head-master Univer School, Louisville; formerly Professor Ancient Languages, Male High School; Author "Fairfax, My Lord," "Outlines of Latin Syntax," etc.

LOUISVILLE KY
JOHN P MORTON & COMPANY
1896

Dedicated to My Wife,

CARY MEADE ALLMOND.
And
MY CHILDREN,

Whose Welfare is " Part and Parcel" of
My Every Thought.

FROM THE LATE PRESIDENT OF
YALE COLLEGE.

Prof. Marcus B. Allmond:

My Dear Sir : Some one was so kind as to send me by post a poem by yourself, entitled "Estelle." Happening to have an hour to spare I at once took it up, and was so interested in it as to read it through at a sitting. I take the liberty to congratulate you as the author of a very lovely idyll, sweet in its spirit, lovely in its pictures, and admirably felicitous in its diction. What can I say more, and I could not say less, if I should say any thing.

Most sincerely yours.

N. PORTER.

New Haven, Conn., June 13, 1884.

PREFACE

SOME years since, when the author was Professor of Ancient Languages in the Male High School, he urged upon the young men of his classes, as an excellent exercise in the acquisition of facility in English expression, a carefully written as well as a painstaking and exact oral translation of the thoughts of the great authors they were reading. He had followed such a course himself at school and at the University of Virginia, and to prove to his pupils that even one without natural gifts might, by such a practice, make some headway in expression, he sat down one Saturday morning, and before the day was over he had finished the most of "Estelle." It embodies, it is true, in the main, experiences had by the author amid the uplands of the Rappahannock, close under the Blue Ridge, in Old Virginia, where at his cousin's home, "Estelle," now the author's wife, was teaching. In some points, however, the story is purely imaginative. It is hardly necessary to tell any one who knows the author that the author is no artist.

(9)

Preface

The art of mixing and handling paints is an enormous mystery to him. And so pronounced are his views against the nefarious liquor traffic that it is equally unnecessary to state that "his breath with wine was" never "strong" at the banquet herein described, or anywhere else, or to declare that he never sang the "Carpe Diem" song. Nor did Mr. William Washington Meade (a nephew of the celebrated Bishop and a grandson of Col. Richard Kidder Meade, of Washington's staff), the father of the author's wife — Virginia Cary Meade — die for many years after "Estelle" was written.

The popularity of the little volume was a genuine surprise to the author, and, when the first edition was exhausted, it was some time before he could make up his mind to publish a second edition. But the thousand copies of the second edition have been exhausted long since — three or four years since — and the demand has seemed so urgent from time to time, that the author is no longer able to resist a third edition, especially as orders have been received from Iowa to California, and from Texas to Massachusetts, and even far-away Germany, within a comparatively short time, showing that the little book has touched a cord that vibrates in the universal heart.

Preface

In the hope that it may bear a blessing to some human soul, that it may shed a bit of sunshine along the pathway of some shadowed life, that it may render pleasurable some hour that otherwise might have been a weary one, that it may bring some heart into closer and sweeter unison with another heart, that it may augment good fellowship and, while more widely diffusing the amenities of life, contribute yet more to the elevation of man and the glory of God, the author commits it for a third time to a generous public. The kind letters it has brought him, the hearty friendships it has made him, the blessèd good-will it has won for him in hearts he never knew, have been to him a source of infinite and abiding pleasure he may not rashly reckon. And when life and its duties are over and death and its mysteries are at hand, it will be one consoling thought that, should all his other efforts at well-doing fail, this one at least has had some measure of success.

In due appreciation of this fact the little volume appears in far handsomer guise than ever before. To the publishers, whose taste in typography is so well known, the author here makes due acknowledgment, and there are others, also, who have considerately assisted him in the habiliment of the poem, to whom he would here return merited thanks,

Preface

were he allowed by them to do so. They must take the wish for the deed. In conclusion, to one and all into whose hands this little book may come the author bids a hearty God-speed in all that is good and true and generous and brave—in all that makes life worth the living and the Far-Beyond an assured and beautiful hope.

Louisville, Ky., December 1, 1896.

ESTELLE

IN that fair land of light and love,
   Where heroes sleep entombed in throngs,
Where laughing skies are blue above
   And Nature sings her sweetest songs —
In that dear land we love and hold
   The saintliest of the sisterhood,
The State of States, whose arms enfold
   Yet hosts on hosts of great and good,
Whose virgin soil bears virgin name,
   Whose best of people wear the grace
Of heirship in their fathers' fame
   With ease that marks a kindred race,
Whose men love honor as their soul,
   And women are Cornelias all,

"A sudden thought now seized on Ned
To weave for her a diadem."

(Page 22)

Estelle

Who count their jewels by the roll
   Of sons who heed their country's call; —
Close nestling under mountains blue
   A streamlet rises in a glen
And makes its way to broader view
   Amid the busier haunts of men;
But ere it leaves its mountain home
   It laughs along fair sloping hills
And catches with its whiter foam
   The ripples of unnumbered rills;
It passes houses, one by one,
   That, nestling 'mid their groves of trees,
Escape the noon-heat of the sun
   When plays the fitful summer breeze;
It passes scenes that would delight
   The painter's or the poet's eye —
That breathe anew by day, by night,
   The glories of an Arcady.
Here in the month of leafy June,
   When roses were in height of pride,

Estelle

And Morning met sweet Afternoon
  And kissed her by the water's side,
The farmer's daughter sits beneath
  The freshness of the maple's shade,
While wild flowers of her native heath
  The balmy airs with fragrance lade.

She caught the lull of noontide hour
  And almost drowsed beside the fell;
The bee had left the rifled flower,
  The sheep had ceased to ring his bell;
The browsing kine forgot to graze
  And stood beneath the trees in dream,
While sunlight flashed its mellow rays
  Upon the bosom of the stream.

The book beside her lay half-shut,
  She floated off on magic seas :
"He comes," she dreams, "he comes ; but, but—"
  Her hair is fingered by the breeze,

Estelle

Ah, well! those lashes, they are long
   And cast their shadows o'er the blue
That now lies hidden (am I wrong?)
   Beneath those lids, just out of view;
And, oh! those cheeks, I know a rose
   Has stolen from its parent-stem
And left the track of tiny toes
   In dimples upon each of them;

And lips, Carnation's own they seem —
   Sweet, dainty lips, the home of bliss —
Such lips as Fancy, in sweet dream,
   Would hover round, yet fear to kiss;
So pure, they seem for angel-words
   The trysting-place and holy shrine,
When with the twitter, as of birds,
   In nuptial joy they intertwine;
And, oh! that chin so neatly turned,
   A Grecian artist, yes, the best,
With silent envy would have burned
   To see the skill it did attest;

Estelle

And brow! it rose a wreath of white
   That bordered wide a wealth of tress
That now in sunny beauty light
   Fell in fair folds upon her dress.
The wanton breeze with lustful glow
   Now freshened as it stroked her hair,
And, as it kissed her brow of snow,
   Declared she was surpassing fair.

She dreamed she saw him on the hill;
   She saw him moving down the path;
She saw him cross the little rill;
   What eyes she dreams her lover hath!
How stately is his form, and fair!
   How strong his step and sure of place!
How wavy his Hyperion hair,
   And what an open, manly face!
But books will often make us dream,
   And June will bring fair fancies up
And tinge them with the mellow gleam
   Of daffodil or buttercup.

Estelle

NOW farmer Creal, a neighbor friend,
While horses to the barn were gone,
Thought it quite well to go (not send)
And see how farmer Rout came on.
Just at his neighbor's gate he met,
A full fourth-mile from house away,
A youth quite fair of mould, who yet
Bore signs of traveling far that day.
Clad in a garb of sober sense,
He seemed to farmer Creal a man
He might address without pretense
Or taking length of time to scan.
"Good-morning!" said the farmer then;
"Good-morning!" said the passer-by.
"Nice day!" the farmer said again;
"Yes, sir," the youth made quick reply,
And added, "Can you tell me, sir,
Where farmer Creal lives hereabout?

Estelle

Or, if he is not living here,
　　Where lives — let's see — old farmer Rout?"
"My name is Creal; and yonder — see!
　　Lives my old friend, good farmer Rout;
I'll take you by his house with me,
　　If you will only turn about."
Then through the gate and down the hill
　　They kept the way that led below,
And chatting, now they cross the rill
　　And reach the spot where maples grow.
And here, oh stay! ye gods above,
　　An Aphrodité, armed in might,
A sunny snare of sunny Love,
　　Breaks in full power upon the sight.
"Estelle's asleep!" the farmer says,
　　And called her: "Estelle, hey, awake!"
Oh! farmers have such sober ways —
　　His ringing words the sweet spell break.
But farmers are the sturdy men
　　That build the nation strong and true,

Estelle

That sink foundations in the fen
  On which we round up to the blue
The house that winds and rains harm not,
  The superstructure that must stand
When you and I are both forgot,
  And children's children own the land.

NOW days went by, as days will do,
  And oft they met, as young folks will,
When air is sweet and skies are blue
  And green grass creeps along the hill.
'Twas afternoon—just such a one
  As June will give beneath the skies
Where Blue Ridge welcomes morning sun
  With her fair, laughing, winsome eyes.
They strolled—Estelle and Ned Holway—
  Along the farm-road up the hill
To where the forest-shadows lay
  In hushed repose, divinely still.

Estelle

He talked in low and quiet wise
  Of men and matters manifold,
And sighed to think the very skies
  Grow brighter if but tinged with gold.
He told the story of his life —
  Of all he dreamed that he would be:
"I've battled there ('twas knife to knife)
  To win an honest victory.
But gold, eternal gold! the cry
  Fills all the world and stays the hand
Of Art, who shrinks back with a sigh
  That greed of gain engulfs the land:
But Art is Art — a thing divine —
  I love her with my very soul;
I'll not forsake her holy shrine
  Till Mammon pay her ample dole."

They now had reached a charming spot,
  Where shade locked hands with shade in glee,
The artist for a while forgot
  The subject of his colloquy.

Photo by W. H. Malone.

* * * She leaned upon his arm
And walked on slowly back toward home,

(Page 26)

Estelle

And now upon a great, wild rock,
    Extending each way many feet,
He piled stone-block upon stone-block
    Until it grew to be a seat
A very queen might love to hold,
    Beneath the overshadowing trees,
And wrapped in vine-leaves crimson-gold,
    Or green as hills by Southern seas.
A honeysuckle wild and red
    Was stretching welcoming hands to them.
A sudden thought now seized on Ned
    To weave for her a diadem.
The violet with blue eyes smiled
    From hiding-place beneath the ledge,
And buttercups were growing wild
    Beyond the sweeping forest's edge.
Now, as he wove, he sprang again
    The subject of an artist's love —
How field and forest, grove and glen,
    And laughing rills and skies above,

Estelle

And all things whisper songs to him,
  And all things seem to woo his heart
To quaff the cup whose mantling brim
  Speaks loyalty to higher art:
"Men's worlds are what they make them — all —
  Or bright or dark or sweet or sad.
Whose heart lets sunshine on it fall
  Or rain-clouds round it battle mad
Has joy or grief as he may choose —
  Has wealth no Crœsus ever knew
Or Poverty that would refuse
  To see the kindness men may do.
For my part I am sworn to seek
  The beauty of God's master-hand;
My art, my tongue, my all shall speak
  The glories of my native land."
And thus he prattled, while a breeze
  Began to stir on hidden wings;
It hummed a low song in the trees
  And toyed with her bonnet-strings.

Estelle

THE SONG OF THE BREEZE.

O, sweet sun-bonnet, lined with pink!
  When June wakes fancies in a youth,
The queenliest bonnet thou, I think,
  That ever circled face of Truth.

O, sweet sun-bonnet, lined with pink!
  O, sweet, fair face just peeping out!
Your dual power would woo, I think,
  And win a heart's last halting doubt.

O, sweet sun-bonnet, lined with pink!
  In whose fair fashion is no art,
But artless art, which is, I think,
  The art of arts to win a heart.

O, sweet sun-bonnet, lined with pink!
  Thou art so witching in thy grace,
My rapt soul lingers lang'rous o'er
  The rose-tints on her lily-face.

Anon she threw it from her brow
  And almost smiled as, looking down,
She saw the artist busy now
  At work upon her floral crown.

" He weaves most well," she thought, "but oh !
   He knows not what he's weaving there,
Two lives —" and then she started so
   Her thought was cleft like brittle ware.
Again she looked upon the crown,
   Again the thought would come, but she
Would struggle so to keep it down —
   "It might, it might be destiny."
And he wove on and talked of art,
   And talked of dreams (we all dream them),
And knew not that he wove his heart
   Into his lady's diadem.

OH ! summer speeds on fairy wings,
   When youth with youth is leagued with Joy ;
And Time counts not the half he brings,
   When tricked in song he plays the boy,
And with round laugh and roguish glee
   Steals smiles from even wrinkled cheeks,

Estelle

And leads a laddie's foot to be
  A truant bold in neighb'ring creeks;
But oh! when sorrow comes between,
  When Grief reclines with pallid brow,
That which was only yestere'en
  Seems ages to both young hearts now.
Oh! wide world o'er, where is the place
  That Death rules not with ruthless sway?
That old, old friend, whose pale, pale face
  Will meet us in some unknown way.
Good farmer Rout in God's own time
  Was called to leave his work and go;
His death you would not call sublime.
  His life was? You would answer, "No."
But silent lives like his, you know,
  Are like the silent work of God,
They teach the grain to sprout and grow,
  They lead the grass on rod by rod
O'er fields where mother Earth lies bare,
  Rough-torn by hand of man or time;

Estelle

And thus they heal the wounds those wear,
  And are more blest than if sublime.
Now, standing at the open grave,
  The artist felt a sorrow new;
He could not tell what 'twas that gave
  Such sympathy as thrilled him through.
He knew a few more days, and then
  His duty called him back to where
He laid aside his work to gain
  A needed rest and wholesome air;
And yet there stirred within his heart
  A tenderness he never owned,
When yonder form seemed reft apart
  By silent Grief that inly moaned,
A noble Impulse rose and said—
  (Ah, well! we'll not repeat it here).
Ambition lifted up her head;
  The Impulse shrank away in fear.

Estelle

A FEW days more, and then by chance
He passed the gate that led within
To Estelle's home. The sun's last glance
  Was resting on this world of sin,
And giving benediction sweet
  In floods of golden, glorious light,
And streaming far away to greet
  The onward coming of the night.
All sorrow-laden she had walked
  On down the roadway to the gate.
They met; before they knew they talked—
  How long we need not here relate.
But, as she leaned upon his arm
  And walked on slowly back toward home,
He felt his heart grow wondrous warm;
  In some strange way his thoughts would roam
To that point where Ambition rose
  And said, "It can not be, and must

Estelle

At once be crushed.   So do n't disclose
  Your weakness to her simple trust."
Estelle was fair, exceeding fair,
  And sorrow gave her yet more grace:
It made more golden yet her hair,
  It made more pretty yet her face;
And then her voice had such a charm,
  It rose and fell in cadence sweet;
And when his eye fell on her arm,
  He found a model quite complete.
Thus moving on, a sudden whir
  Of wings, and then before their eyes
A young bird fell, (was it not queer?)
  And, wounded, struggled hard to rise.
Estelle was touched, and said, "Poor thing,
  A cruel hand has wrought thee wrong;
A bird that bears a broken wing
  Can never sing its sweetest song."
And that was all; the artist knew
  To-morrow he must leave, if he

"Far from the busy haunts of men
Is maiden meditative now."

Photo by W. H. Malone.

(Page 34)

Estelle

Would step by step rise upward through
  Temptation to art's mastery.

TO-MORROW came, and he was gone;
  And she — well, women can be strong.
A dream that they have dreamt upon
  Until it works almost a wrong,
They yet can hide away and smile,
  And none of those they chance to meet
Can ever know how they beguile
  Their hearts to play such fair deceit.

THE artist stood within his room
  And worked at easel long and stout.
From morning's light to evening's gloom
  Fair ladies went within, without.
And one there was who often came
  And watched the paintings as they grew;
And with her was a stately dame
  Whose diamonds flashed upon the view.

Estelle

There was no doubt but wealth was theirs;
   There was no further doubt but they
Were not so wrapped in art affairs
   That oft their eyes would stray away
To where the artist, deep in thought,
   Was linking dream to dream so fair
That all about him, as he wrought,
   He fancied was ambrosial air.
In time he met with them and grew
   To know they were sweet Fashion's own,
Whose art levees a parvenu
   Regarded as quite near the throne.
Ambition stirred anew within
   His heart of hearts, as now he read
The work he need not to begin,
   If he would yield but to be led.
The way was plain, the sailing clear,
   The world would then all honor give;
With talent, wealth, and fashion near,
   He well might think it sweet to live.

Estelle

He looked his gallery round, and saw
  'Twas here an eye, 'twas there a hand,
That seemed in some strange way to draw
  His thoughts unto another land,
And mountains blue and sunny skies,
  And golden locks in wavy fold,
And all the depth of blue in eyes,
  And memories of the days of old.

'Twas cruel to his name to dream
  Of turning from this chance away.
As Fashion's favorites round did stream,
  When night had intercepted day,
He felt a very lord of men,
  A monarch of a little world;
And round and round, again, again,
  In mazy dance his glad heart whirled.
The blazing diamonds sparkled bright,
  The slippered feet in kid were clad,
And surely never revel-wight
  A more enlisted partner had.

Estelle

She threw her soul into the dance,
　And seemed enkindled with the throng,
As foot to foot and glance to glance
　Their airy figures flashed along.
But, O! there was, I can not tell,
　A little something wanting yet
To win him, and to win him well,
　So well that he must needs forget.

No ties now bound him to that lass,
　That little country-maiden there;
He simply met her as you pass
　A rose-bush flowering in the air;
You stop and view the roses red,
　You catch the perfume with your breath,
And then you stride on straight ahead
　And care not how they meet their death.
This world is all a thing of show,
　And who would ride upon the crest
Must rate these finer feelings low,
　And not be hampered or distrest.

Estelle

If birds with broken wings should fall
    Before his feet with plaintive look,
He casts them from the way, that's all;
    They'll find some little, hidden nook.
Thus did Ambition lure his soul
    And find a reason for each act:
We go to pieces on the shoal
    In fleeing from the cataract.

OH! such is life; and ere we know
    'Tis presto! and a change is made,
And what was *this* a while ago,
    Is *that* before it can be said.
And so, within that distant glen
    Beneath the mountain's arching brow,
Far from the busy haunts of men,
    Is maiden meditative now.
She sees the sun rise in the east,
    She sees the sun set in the west,
She sees the Summer spread her feast,
    And Autumn come a welcome guest.

Estelle

Her daily round of duties all —
　Her books, her walks, her dreams by night —
Are shadowed by an inward pall
　Whose edges gleam with golden light;
For, though the face of Hope was hid,
　Faith, loving maid that knows no guile,
In dreamless innocency bid
　Her heart play with a wanton wile.
The flowers knew her kindly touch,
　The bird's poor broken wing was healed,
The lambs all grew to love her much,
　And followed faithful round the field;
The trees swung out their hands in glee,
　The brooklets laughed as she passed on
The breezes breathed in ecstacy,
　The sun rays welcomed her at morn.
She taught the music now to stray
　In winsome grace o'er pliant strings,
And oft she sang a roundelay
　That ran into more serious things:

Estelle

HER SONG.

Ah! hope is mine, and hope is well,
  And work will keep her young heart sweet;
The morn shall find me down the dell,
  The night shall give me rest complete.
Ah! hope is mine, and hope is well,
  And work will keep her young heart sweet.

Ah! hope is mine, and hope is well,
  But clouds will linger in the sky;
I wonder if they will not swell
  And burst in tempests by and by.
Ah! hope is mine, and hope is well,
  But clouds will linger in the sky.

Ah! hope is mine, and hope is well,
  And work will keep her young heart sweet.
I do not know, I can not tell
  Which way she leads my willing feet;
But hope is mine, and hope is well,
  And work will keep her young heart sweet.

Estelle

And, suiting action then to song,
  She took her life up new again,
And bore it like a lark along
  The by-paths of that little glen.
As chance now opened up the way,
  She taught the children in the school.
(How easy is a teacher's sway
  Where Love is law, and Duty, rule.)
She grew to have exalted aim;
  She saw within their little eyes,
All nicely set within its frame,
  A picture of sweet Paradise;
And knew that each pure little heart
  Was in itself a costly gem,
And were it nurtured quite apart
  Would stud the Master's diadem.
But man is man's supremest foe,
  Though he should be his dearest friend,
And thousands league for brothers' woe
  While hundreds work for better end.

Photo by W. L. Bresee.

Estelle

The Cæsars of this cruel earth
  Have been the spoilers of the best
That God's dear love has wooed to birth
  In every human being's breast.
Man preys upon his fellow-man,
  And children in their very teens,
While learning use of *a* or *an*,
  Interpolate a thousand scenes
Of Life's kaleidoscopic round
  Upon the neighbor children's soul;
And thus the serpent's track is bound
  By Human-life's concentric whole.
She thought if she could lead them out
  And let the hills speak to them words
And airs of heaven lap them 'bout
  And glad them with the songs of birds,
And there along the brooklet's banks
  The story of the waters teach,
She might accord herself due thanks
  For keeping them from Harm's sad reach.

Estelle

So, often when the tasks were o'er,
   And books were laid aside that day,
She led them gently from the door
   Across the field and forest way;
She taught them of the beauties sweet
   That lay on hill-side and in vale,
That fell about their very feet
   And rose in joy to regale;
She told them that the human soul
   Is like a wondrous mirror made,
And will reflect the half or whole,
   In fuller light or deeper shade,
Of all this joyous universe,
   That speaks of beauty, truth, and God,
And be the better or the worse
   Upon a human will's mere nod.
If it is worn as it should be,
   And kept undimmed by sin's foul breath,
It will reflect the harmony
   That moves through all things — even death.

Estelle

She led them then from self to stray,
  And begged them walk with open eyes
And watch for flowers along the way,
  And hand in hand ascend the rise;
She told them earth was rich and sweet,
  That God looks outward from the skies.
If man his fellow man would greet
  With warmth of heart and loving eyes,
Old Want would fold her hands and sleep,
  And Crime into a dwarf would shrink,
And Sorrow's heart would cease to weep,
  And fell Despair halt on the brink.
A great warm heart will burgeon out,
  If Faith and Charity are there,
But greed of gain is seed of doubt,
  And doubt will nurture sin and care.
It is not what we have, but are,
  That makes us happy here on earth,
And up beyond or sun or star
  Our souls are reckoned as our worth.

Estelle

As air pours in a tainted room
  And sweeps the pestilence away,
And to the wan restores the bloom,
  And for the darkness gives the day,
So Nature peeps into the heart
  And blows the bloom of roses in,
And swings the dusky doors apart
  And sweeps away the brood of sin.

But, oh! the teacher as she taught
  Yet grew and grew more lovely still,
And far the noblest work she wrought
  Was this — she schooled a perfect will.
And though she sometimes dreamed "Perhaps,"
  She smiled and said "God knoweth best."
And while the children conned their maps,
  Her lily heart had perfect rest.

Estelle

THE world had seized him, and he flung
　　His ardent heart into the stream;
He rose a meteor, that now hung
　　In mid-air as the planets seem.
His friends were scores on scores, and they
　　Hung round him with a hollow glee,
And made the midnight hour like day
　　With song and dance and revelry.
The club-rooms gleamed with golden light,
　　The banquet table groaned with freight;
To round the hour of waning night,
　　The wine-cup sat beside the plate.
They each had sung a little song —
　　They all had spoken each his speech,
The artist's breath with wine was strong,
　　As back he leaned with glass in reach.

Estelle

HIS SONG: CARPE DIEM.

Brave Caecuban and Massic clear!
  Horatian strains will celebrate,
With old Falernian, year by year,
  Your powers to intoxicate!
But whether it be Caecuban,
  Or Massic mantling to the brim,
Or glorious old Falernian,
  Who drinks the deepest, here's to him!

Oh! Bacchus wears the poplar wreath,
  And Venus smiles with sweet delight:
Come! gather now out, boys, beneath
  The stars that gem the brow of night,
And let us sing a roundelay
  And round it up with measure trim,
And drain the wine-cup while we may,
  Who drinks the deepest, here's to him!

A merry song, come one, come all,
  Let Cytherea lead the dance;
And, while the Graces are in call,
  Let's bring them forth as each may chance;
And, while Apollo we salute,
  Amid the Muses, tricked and prim,

Estelle

With glass to glass and foot to foot,
  Who drinks the deepest, here's to him!

Ah! Time flies fast and soon is gone;
  We buried Yesterday at night.
To-morrow will have come and flown
  Almost before it seems in sight.
Then seize the day; let mirth flow on.
  Our chance for length of life is slim.
Once more, before the day shall dawn,
  Who drinks the deepest, here's to him!

The seed of wine is seed of wrong,
  And seed of wrong will fruit in ill;
And, though you wait the harvest long,
  You may expect the harvest still.
Old Nature is a kindly dame,
  And keeps her plenty on the shelf,
But she will yet assert her claim
  In due time to protect herself.
Outraged, she grows terrific then,
  And wreaks her vengeance manifold;

Estelle

You may not coax her to her den,
  You may not bribe her off with gold.
Long days the fever dread had raged,
  Its ebb-tide now was setting in,
And kind attendants all presaged
  That time and hope the fight would win.
As in these sluggish after-hours
  He lay and languished in his bed,
There came a little bunch of flowers
  In which were honeysuckles red,
And violets with eyes all blue,
  And buttercups all creamy gold;
And then there burst upon his view
  The memories of the days of old.
There was no word to tell the tale
  Of friendship lingering through the years—
There was no plea—no storm—no gale—
  No burst of passion—flood of tears;
And yet his soul was through and through
  Thrilled as by hidden battery's shock;

Estelle

His own sweet thoughts stormed into view,
  And smote with might the desert rock.
And then he recognized as true
  In all the round of life's fair things
The fairest (ah! need I tell you?)
  Was where the Rappahannock springs.
And, as the days passed slowly on,
  There grew upon the canvas there,
As bit by bit from morn to morn
  He worked to drive away dull care,
A picture of a forest-queen,
  With crown of wild flowers on her head,
High-throned on rocks—-a living green
  With moss whose soft plush carpeted
The tesselated floor beneath,
  Which won a deeper tinge from trees
Whose locked arms longed to make bequeath
  Of trysting spot to love and ease.
He caught the sun-ray's laughing light,
  And locked it in her golden hair;

Estelle

He set the lily's seal of white
  Upon her face and features fair;
He won the rosebud's pouting grace
  And on her arching lips it grew;
Rose petals on her cheeks found place,
  And in her eyes were violets blue.
And now the dawn seemed broken sweet
  In whelming freshness o'er all lands,
As ever more and more complete
  Expression grew beneath his hands.
It was a picture that would stay
  A very Vulcan, if not blind,
It was a picture, I must say,
  Whose canvas was the artist's mind.
For he was feeble many days,
  And like a very infant weak;
His hand with effort he could raise,
  His voice almost forgot to speak.

Then came a letter. Farmer Creal
  Thought rest among the mountains good,

"If he could teach himself to feel
    Content with pure air and plain food;"
And Cousin Mary (Creal's good wife)
    Must add a post-script just to say
"You must come, Ed. Upon my life
    We'll cure you. Yours, devoted, May."
Oh! farmers' wives are oft so kind
    Up 'mid those dear old mountains blue,
They'll ransack all the house to find
    Some better way of serving you.

'TWAS eventide — that holy hour
    When calm invests the realms of air,
And dew brings joy unto the flower
    Whose head is drooping in despair.
The stars were in the silent sky,
    The soft light fell on hill and dale,
The meadow brook went purling by
    The clover-blooms that filled the vale;

Estelle

The fire-flies hung above the meads
  Like ships of airy little sprites,
And wreathed with threads of golden beads
  The dark hair of this queen of nights.
Afar, anear, there was a hush
  Unbroken, save at intervals
When nightingales upon the bush
  Burst into lovely madrigals.
The artist at the window-side
  Reclined upon the settee's length,
Looked out upon the prospect wide
  And drank with every breath new strength.
The mountains in the distance now
  Were growing brighter as there rose
The moon in silence o'er their brow
  And smiled upon the earth's repose.
" To-morrow," queried he, " and then?
  Ah ! then the Rubicon is passed ;
For me as for the rest of men
  The die for once and all is cast."

Estelle

To-morrow woke from out of sleep
   And cast her night-robes from her breast,
And from the hill-tops tried to peep
   On that sweet vale's unbroken rest;
But soon the birds with silver throat
   Bade welcome to her coming feet,
And Nature added note to note
   Until the chorus was complete;
The sheep stirred on the hill-tops green,
   The cattle browsed beside the stream,
The milk-maid moved the cows between,
   The farm-hand harnessed up his team.
The sun arose in austere pride,
   And beamed upon the wakened world;
By every streamlet's laughing side
   Peace's white-winged banner was unfurled;
The dew-drop on the clover-leaf
   Like some pure maiden felt his breath,
His beamy joy but brought her grief,
   His kiss was but the kiss of death.

Estelle

The artist found himself e'er noon
  Down at the widow's modest home;
Ah! who can stay in-doors when June
  With witching smiles suggests a roam.
They made their way as long before
  (Old habit is old habit still)
From out the parlor to the door,
  Then up the farm-road to the hill.
He had already told her of
  The rich fulfillment of his dreams,
But now he seemed somehow to love
  To dwell upon such pleasant themes;
He spoke of how he hoped his health
  Would soon allow him to return
And with new fame get greater wealth
  Than he had yet essayed to earn;
He spoke of how his city home
  Was hung with pictures — all his own —
Of how his friends should often come
  And spend the evenings there alone.

Estelle

Now, as they wandered up the hill,
  They reached a spot where great trees rise,
The breeze grew fresh and fresher still,
  And bluer grew the deep blue skies.
Without forethought, Estelle now sat
  ('T was such a charming scene below)
Right on the ledge, still gazing at
  The harvesters move to and fro;
The wheat-field stretched out far and wide,
  The golden grain, like inland seas,
Now flowed in ebb, now rose in tide,
  Wave chasing wave as breeze chased breeze.
The bob-white whistled on the rail,
  The harvesters broke into song,
And now, across the pretty vale
  The wheat-shocks ranged themselves along.
The artist knew the hour was there —
  The moment of supreme suspense —
His love he must at once declare
  And yet could find no good pretense.

Estelle

He had been brave for many things,
   He had been bold at other hours,
But now his courage lost her wings
   And speech seemed reft of all her powers.
It may be that he felt his life
   Depended for its weal or woe
On whether she would be his wife,
   Or, self-sufficient, give him " no "—
And "yes," or "no," he could not tell.

   Had he seen less of man and man's,
He might have guessed it very well
   And trusted to his heart's sweet plans.
But he had seen a woman smile
   So oft within that world without,
That *he* had grown to place a guile
   Where *she* would never dream a doubt.
But little things will often give
   Excuse for great wide-sweeping acts,
And empires often rise and live
   On pretexts that have murdered facts.

"A bunch of wild flowers often can
Decide the destiny of man.

(Page 54)

Estelle

His eye fell on the violets blue,

    The honeysuckle's breath was sweet,

And buttercups just yonder grew

    Where field and neighb'ring forest meet.

A bunch of wild flowers often can,

    When youth in joy is leagued with youth,

Decide the destiny of man —

    Between the lines you read the truth,

Or should ; for up the hill they went

    With strange forebodings on their part,

And down they came, and sweet Content

    Was coyly nestling in each heart.

A WELL-BELOVED and loving home

    Is God's own picture of the blest —

A spot to which, where'er we roam,

    We all may turn and find sweet rest.

If, busy at his studio,

    The artist worked the livelong day,

Estelle

He knew the shades of night would throw
  The light of home about his way.
A man's love wavers to and fro,
  Yet settles down at last in strength;
A woman's love, as women go,
  Is love unto love's fullest length;
And he that has it, has what he
  Should value as his very soul —
A buoy that upon life's sea
  Is strongest when the tempests roll;
But, oh! when woman's love is God's,
  And sweetened by that higher good,
Its influence reaches many rods,
  And consecrates a neighborhood;
She is a city on a hill —
  A light that never can be hid.
Her husband feels her gentle will,
  The child will love, should she forbid.
And Estelle sits at eventide
  With ease and plenty all about,

Estelle

And, in a little crib beside,
  A baby-foot kicks in and out,
And now she bends, and with her hand
  Plays with its little 'broidered gown
Or gives a kiss or ties a band
  Or smoothes its golden ringlets down.
It cooes and laughs and lifts its fist,
  And kicks its little toes in air,
And now — what mother can resist?
  She bounds with baby down the stair
And open throws the door, and then —
  A kiss for her, and baby, too,
Behold· the happiest now of men.
  They enter, and are gone from view.

L'ENVOY.

O, men that work and men that bear!
  What gives you grace to work and wait?
The morning kiss upon the stair,
  The evening welcome at the gate.

www.ingramcontent.com/pod-product-compliance
Lightning Source LLC
Chambersburg PA
CBHW031321280626
47169CB00019B/2568

* 9 7 8 3 3 3 7 3 7 0 6 1 9 *